I0719692

what if mermaids are real?

what if they live so far down in the depths of the ocean that we just can't see them?

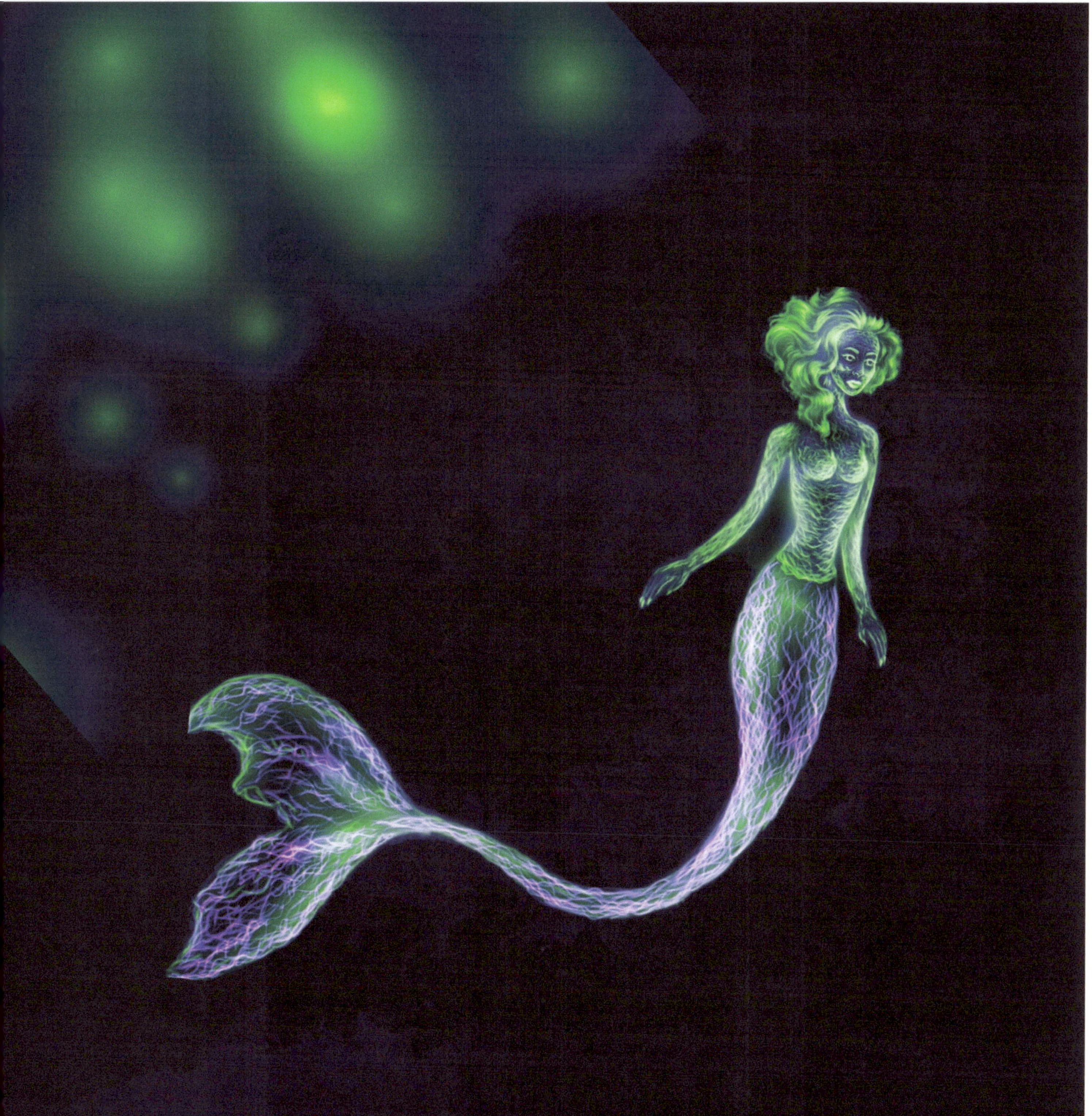

with the depths being so dark, maybe the mermaids would look ghostly – or at least iridescent.

Do they live alone or do they function better as a society, living together cohesively and looking out for one another?

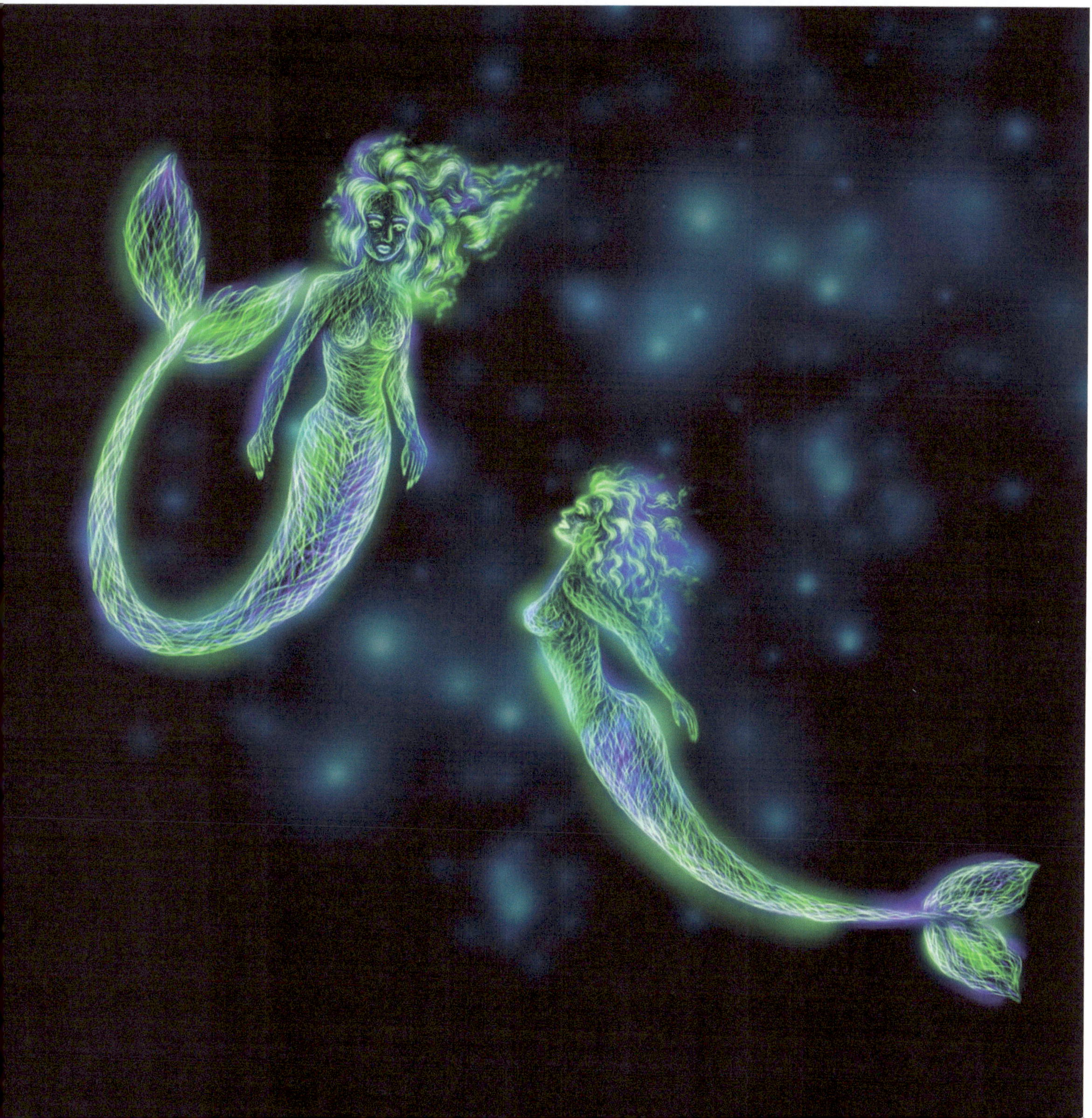

Would they have leaders?
And maybe even subordinates?

would they have magical powers?

Or would it perhaps be more complex than that?

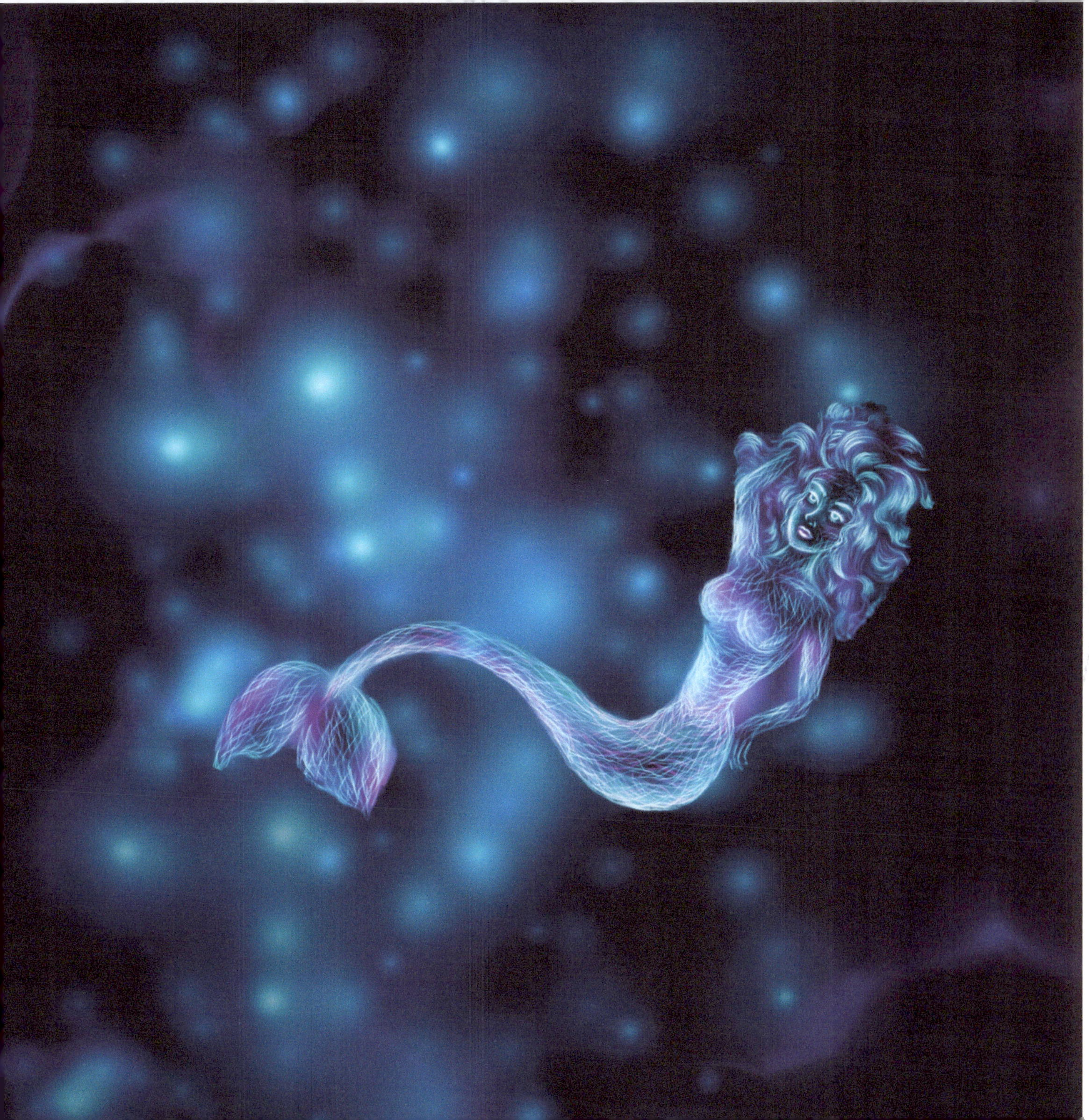

With so much down there, in the dark depths of the sea, we'll never get to see it all.

So surely it's plausible that
mermaids could be real?

What if they're more ghostly than human-like? Could they be lost souls who roam not the earth, not the heavens, but the very depths of the sea?

what if we ever got to meet them?
would they be pleased to see us?
Or would they be livid at being
disturbed? Or perhaps feeling
scared, they'd just swim away.

If mermaids are real, then why haven't we seen them yet?

Equally though, do we need proof, to believe they exist?

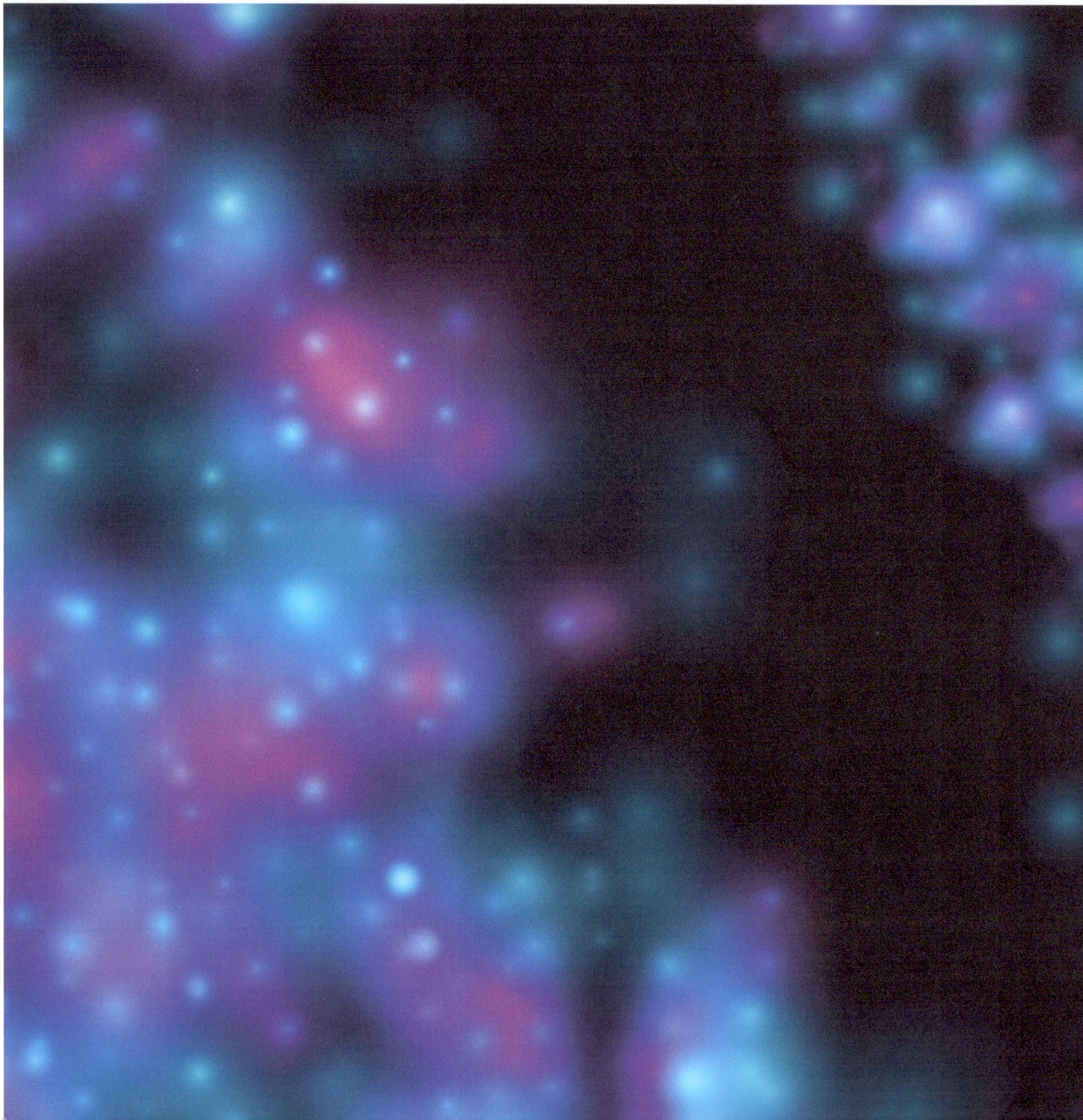